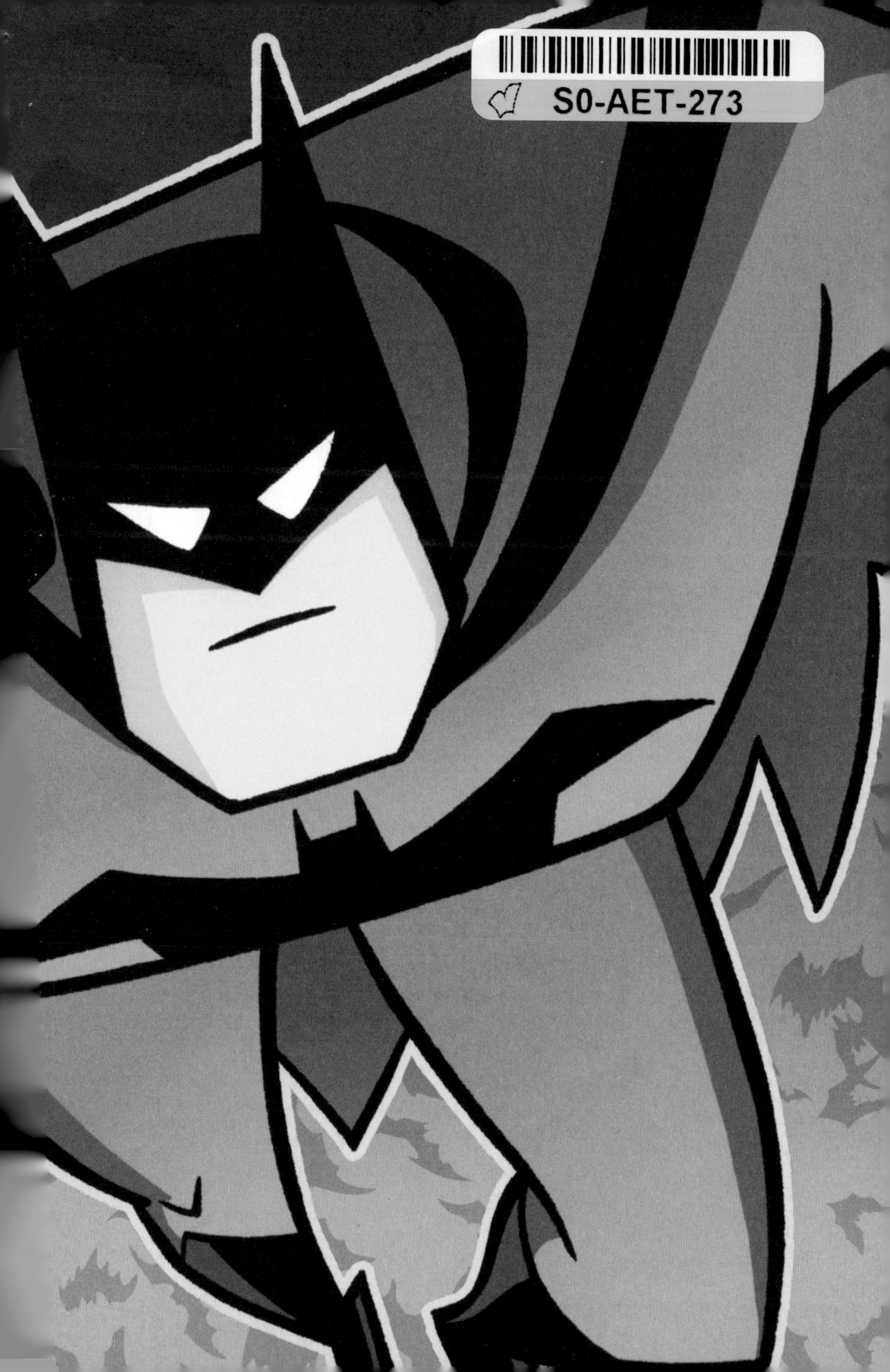

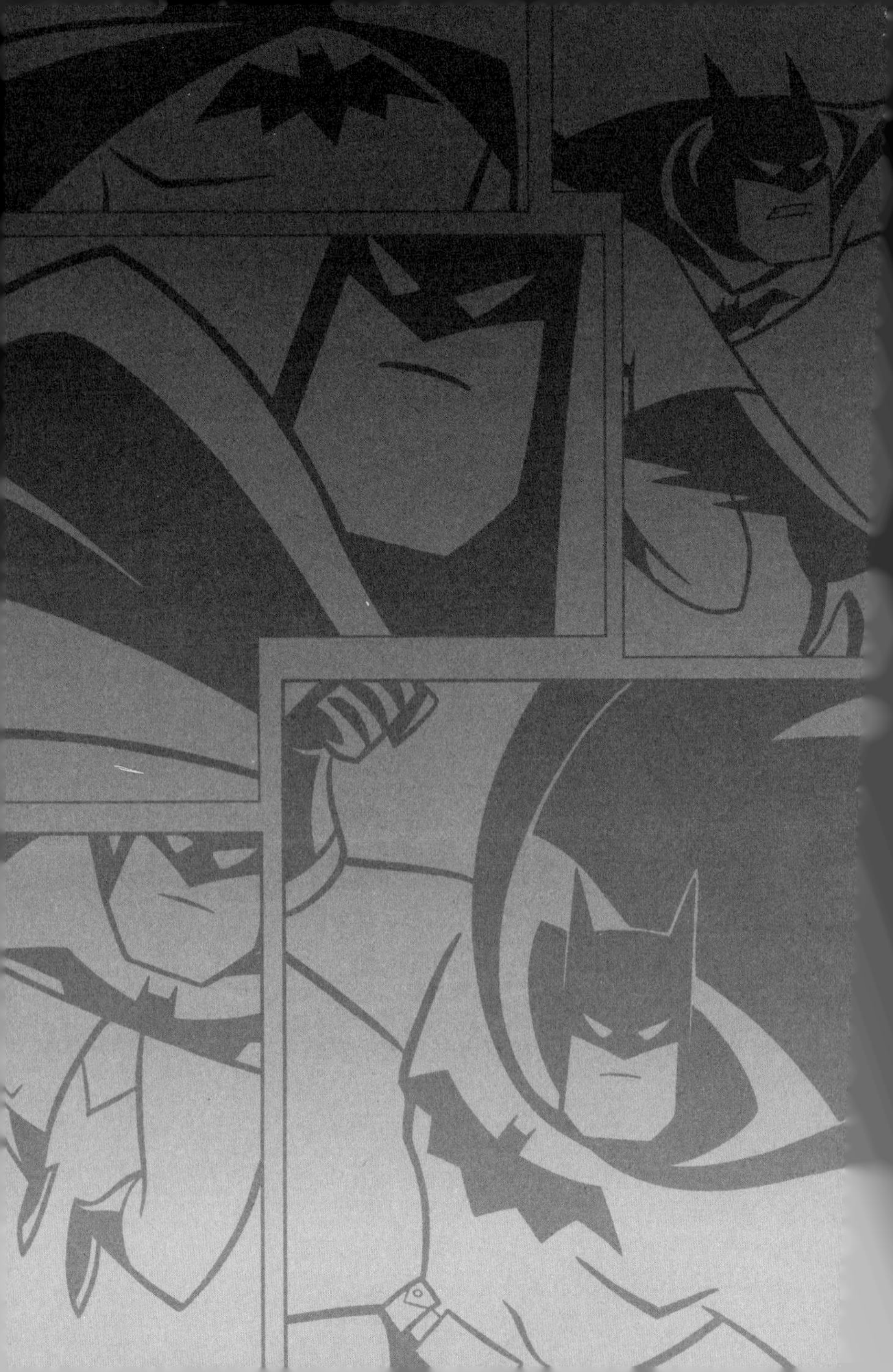

SUPER **DC** HEROES

BATMAN

FUN HOUSE OF EVIL

WRITTEN BY
DONALD LEMKE

ILLUSTRATED BY
ERIK DOESCHER,
MIKE DeCARLO, AND
DAVID TANGUAY

BATMAN CREATED BY
BOB KANE

STONE ARCH BOOKS
MINNEAPOLIS   SAN DIEGO

Published by Stone Arch Books in 2009
151 Good Counsel Drive, P.O. Box 669
Mankato, Minnesota 56002
www.stonearchbooks.com

Library of Congress Cataloging-in-Publication Data
Lemke, Donald B.
    Fun House of Evil / by Donald Lemke; illustrated by Erik Doescher.
    p. cm. — (DC Super Heroes. Batman)
    ISBN 978-1-4342-1145-3 (library binding)
    ISBN 978-1-4342-1367-9 (pbk.)
    [1. Superheroes—Fiction.] I. Doescher, Erik, ill. II. Title.
PZ7.L53746Fu 2009
[Fic]—dc22   2008032404

Summary: The Joker escapes from Arkham Asylum and tricks Batman
into following him into an old warehouse. But the building has been
remodeled into the Joker's fun house. Batman must outwit clown robots
and escape deadly amusement rides to make sure that the Joker does not
have the last laugh!

Art Director: Bob Lentz
Designer: Bob Lentz

1 2 3 4 5 6 14 13 12 11 10 09

TABLE OF CONTENTS

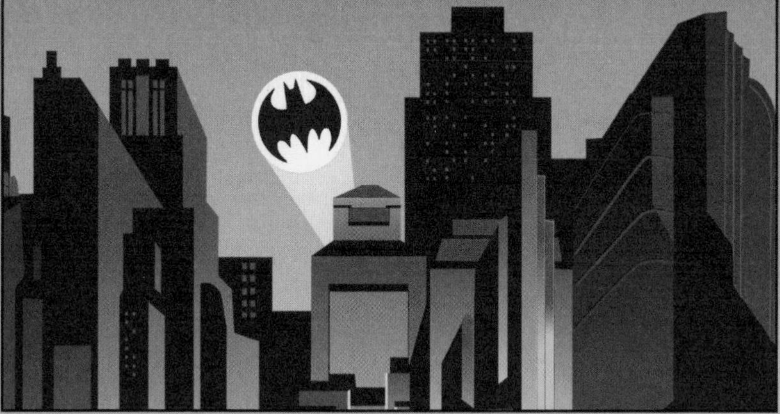

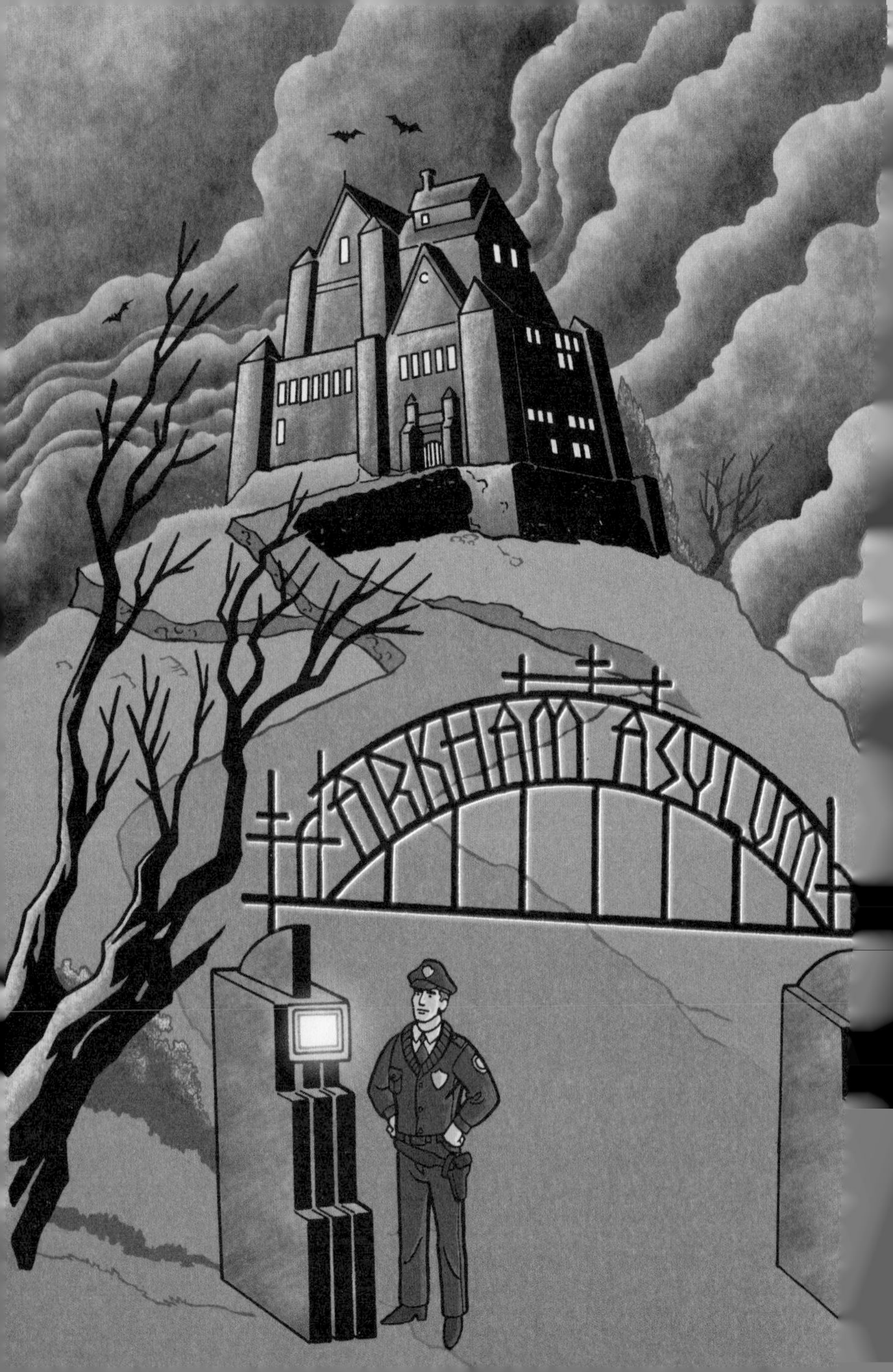
ARKHAM ASYLUM

CHAPTER 1

SPECIAL DELIVERY

As a dark rain began to fall, the squad car reached the entrance of Arkham Asylum. Locked behind the gates were some of the world's most dangerous criminals. And tonight, the worst of all would finally be joining them.

"Special delivery from the Gotham City Police Department," said Officer Roder into the security speaker.

"What do you have for us tonight?" a crackly voice replied.

"He calls himself the Joker. But I doubt he'll be laughing for a while," the officer said. He glanced back at the squad car. His prisoner sat quietly in the shadows of the backseat.

Just then, lightning flashed in the sky. The Joker's face glowed with an eerie grin. It sent shivers down the officer's spine.

"Pull ahead," said the voice from the speaker. "Our guard will meet you at the front door."

As the heavy gates opened, the officer got back in the squad car. For a moment the car didn't move. Then suddenly, its engine roared.

VROOOOOM! VROOOOOM!

The wheels began to spin on the wet road. The car raced up the windy hill. It blared its sirens and shined its warning lights.

Seconds later, the squad car screeched to a stop in front of the asylum. "What's the big rush?" the guard asked the driver.

"Just got a call from headquarters," the man in the front seat replied. "Can you take over from here?"

"No problem," said the guard. He opened the rear door of the squad car. He yanked out the passenger.

The angry prisoner kicked and struggled. He moaned through a piece of tape that now covered his mouth.

"What's with the tape?" the guard asked.

"Had to shut him up," said the man. He revved the car's engine. "But don't worry. He's not such a bad guy! Hahaha!"

The squad car squealed back down the hill. The laughter faded. Standing outside the asylum, the prisoner now struggled and moaned even louder.

"Okay, okay," said the guard. He grabbed the tape on the prisoner's mouth. When he pulled, a white rubber mask slipped off the head of Officer Roder.

"You fool!" yelled Officer Roder. His face was red and sweating. "Call Commissioner Gordon. The Joker has escaped!"

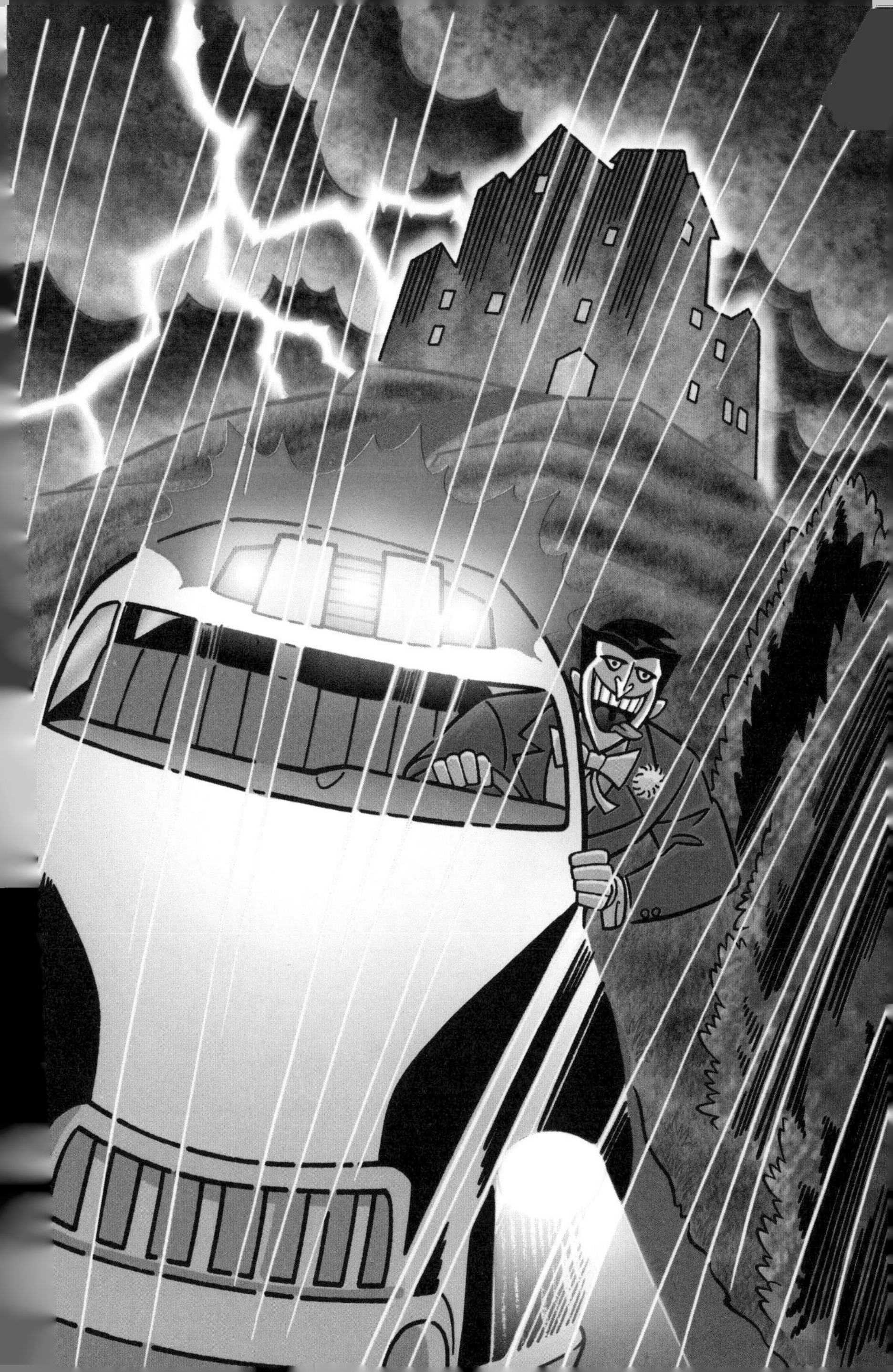

CHAPTER 2

PREPARE THE BATMOBILE!

A few miles north near the Gotham city limits, laughter filled the Wayne Manor ballroom. Inside the mansion, dozens of the city's richest citizens gathered to celebrate.

"Happy birthday, Bruce!" a man in a tuxedo shouted. He raised his glass above the crowd. "Here's to many more fabulous years!" The other guests raised their glasses as well. They cheered for their host.

Bruce Wayne stood at the bottom of the mansion's grand staircase. He nodded politely. Then he headed up the stairs.

As the party continued below, Bruce sank into a chair next to his bedroom window. He flicked on the lamp. Bruce grabbed a picture off a nearby table. Then he let out a deep sigh.

The butler poked his head around the bedroom door. "Is everything all right, Master Bruce?" he asked.

"Yes, Alfred, everything's fine," Bruce replied. He didn't look up.

Alfred moved closer. He looked at the picture Bruce was holding. The faded image showed young Bruce standing with his parents in front of a Ferris wheel. Each of them was smiling. They were trying to hold onto a group of colorful balloons.

"Ah yes, I remember that day," said Alfred.

"You were there?" asked Bruce.

"I took the picture," he replied. "It was your birthday. The year before your mother and father were —"

"Murdered," Bruce interrupted.

Alfred placed his hand on Bruce's shoulder. "Of course, sir," he said. "I have never forgotten the past."

Suddenly, outside the bedroom window, a bright light shined in the darkened sky. Bruce and Alfred looked out at the glowing circle. It held the shadow of a bat inside. They both knew exactly what the signal meant.

"I've never forgotten either," said Bruce. "Prepare the Batmobile!"

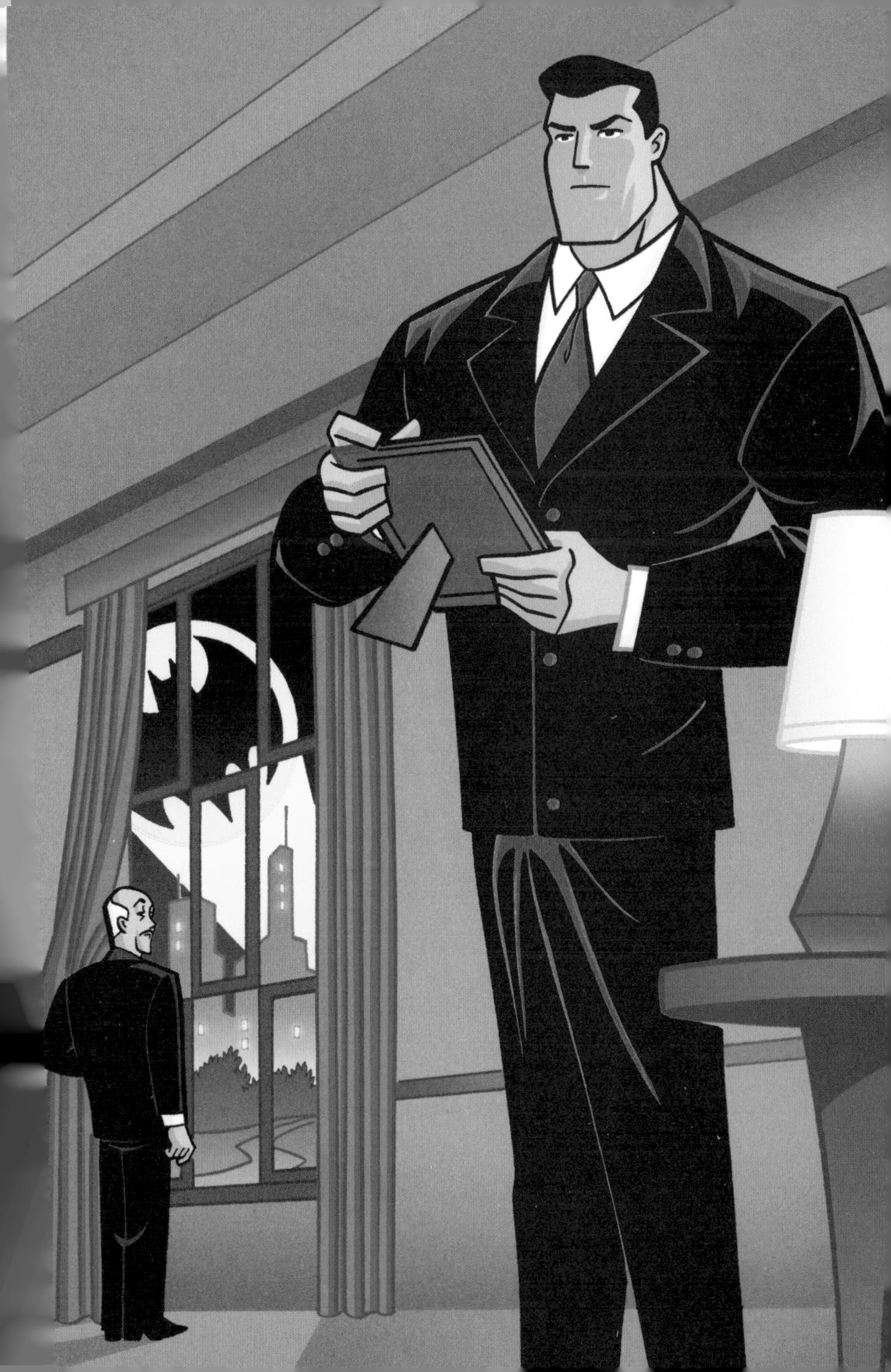

Moments later, Bruce rushed through the secret passage to the Batcave. The cave was hidden deep below the mansion. It contained everything needed for his transformation into Batman, the Dark Knight of Gotham City.

Bruce changed into the Batsuit. Alfred called Commissioner Gordon. Then he updated Batman on the situation.

"It appears the Joker has escaped, sir," Alfred said. "Commissioner Gordon would like you to meet him at the asylum."

Batman slid into the driver's seat of the Batmobile. He switched on the vehicle's computer. The dashboard lit up with a hundred switches and lights. The engine thundered like a jet, ready to take off.

VROOOOM!!

"Sir, what shall I tell the guests?" asked Alfred.

Batman hit a switch to open the Batcave's secret exit. He smiled. "Tell them I'm taking out some trash."

•　•　•

Within minutes, the Batmobile arrived at Arkham. Outside, dozens of Gotham City police officers searched the scene for clues.

"I hope I didn't interrupt anything, Batman," said Police Commissioner James Gordon. "But our friend, the Joker, left a little message for you."

He handed Batman the mask that the Joker had used to escape. Batman stared at its evil grin and wild green hair.

Batman flipped the mask around. He noticed a message scribbled inside: "See you soon, Batman! Your pal, the Joker."

"How thoughtful," said Batman.

"What do you make of it?" asked Commissioner Gordon.

The Dark Knight snipped a piece of rubber from the mask. He placed it inside a small kit that he removed from his Utility Belt. The kit's monitor flashed through a series of graphs. Then it stopped.

"Hmmm. The chemical in this white paint is highly unusual. It's also highly toxic," said Batman. "The factory that made it was shut down years ago."

"So what do we do now?" asked the commissioner.

"Take care of your officer," said Batman. He pointed toward Officer Roder. "He's about to get one nasty rash. As for me, I'm going to solve the mystery behind this mask."

CHAPTER 3

JOKER'S FUN HOUSE

Back inside the Batmobile, the Dark Knight switched on the afterburners.

WHOOOOSH!

He raced through the streets of Gotham. As he neared an area known as Crime Alley, the Batmobile slowed to a stop.

The rundown factory nearby appeared to be closed, just as Batman had suspected. Even so, he decided to check it out.

The Dark Knight walked closer to the factory. He read a large sign on the front door: *Danger! Chemicals are flammable!*

Then he heard noises coming from the boarded windows. It sounded like music and laughter.

This has to be a trap, he thought. *Luckily, I like surprise parties.*

Batman grabbed the tool kit from his Utility Belt. Using his electro lock-picking device, he unbolted a steel chain. Then he slowly opened the front door. The factory was dark. The music had stopped. Batman switched on his night-vision lenses and stepped inside.

The metal doors closed quickly behind him.

Suddenly, the room exploded with spinning and twirling neon lights. Bells, whistles, and music screamed from every direction. Batman buckled in pain. He covered his ears against the throbbing noises. Before he could recover, something hit his legs from behind.

He fell backward into a small, moving cart. Looking around, Batman realized he was on some sort of roller coaster. The roller coaster cart was speeding forward along a wooden track.

"What's going on?" he shouted.

"Comfortable, Batboy?" a loud voice roared through the factory.

"Joker!" yelled Batman. "Where are you?"

"Wouldn't you rather like to know where *you* are?" the Joker replied. "Welcome to my Fun House of Evil!"

"Sounds great, Clown. But I've had enough fun for one evening," Batman said.

CLANK! CLANK!

Two steel handcuffs locked around Batman's wrists. He twisted and turned. He struggled to get free.

CLANK! CLANK!

Two more metal shackles shot up from the floor. They snapped shut around Batman's ankles. He was trapped!

"Please keep your hands and feet inside the ride at all times," yelled the Joker. "Hahaha!"

The Joker's laugh echoed through the factory. The ride picked up speed. It weaved back and forth down the twisted track. Batman stared into the darkness.

Suddenly, the cart began to shake. A giant metal clown face burst out of the floor ahead. The face rose twenty feet into the air. Fireworks shot out from its ears. Flames spewed from its nose. Then the mouth opened. Inside the mouth was a deep tunnel and a giant set of teeth.

CHOMP! CHOMP! CHOMP!

The mouth crunched down again and again. The ride sped up even more.

CHOMP! CHOMP! CHOMP!

The tracks led right into the jaws of the deadly clown.

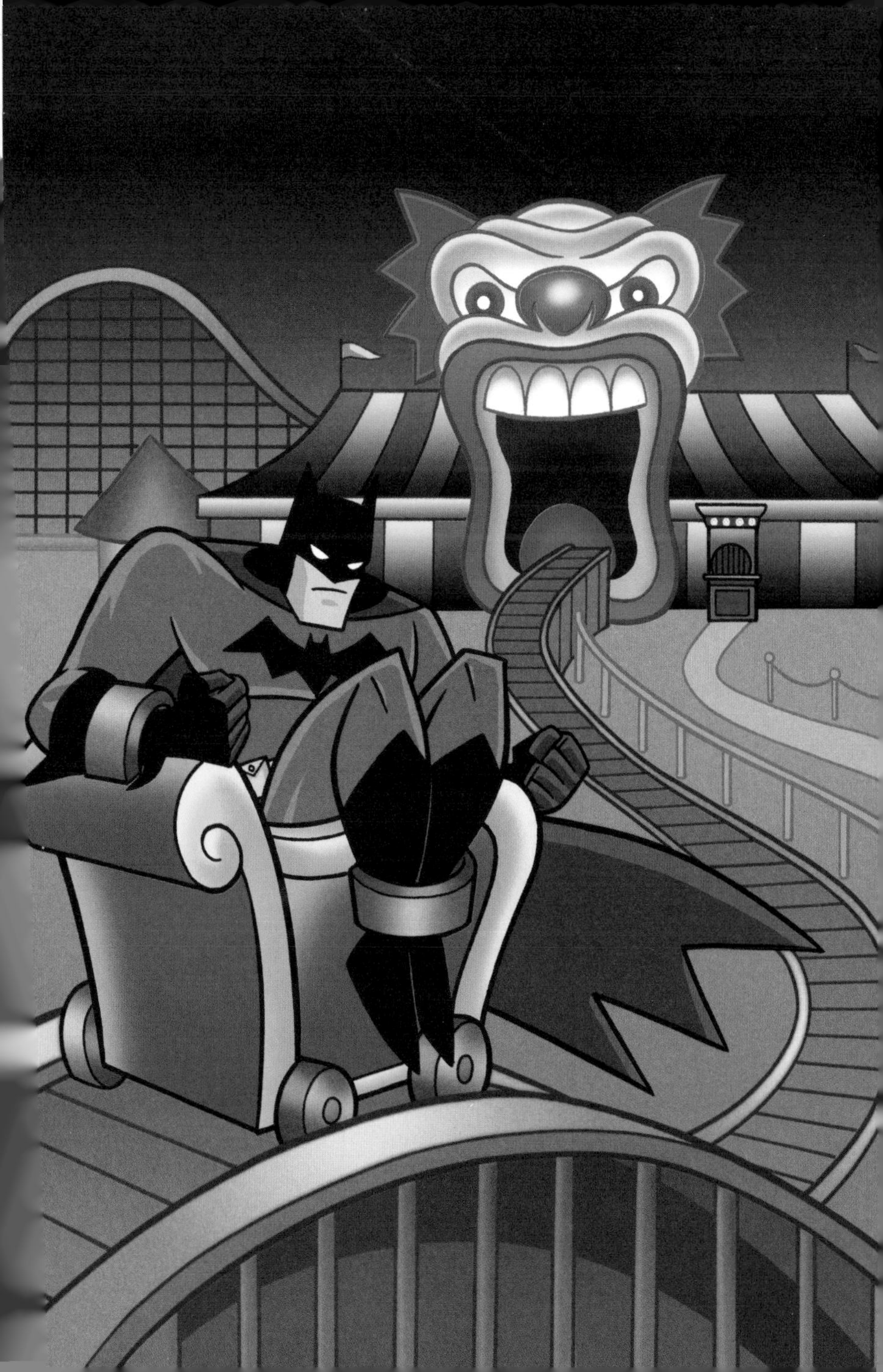

Batman struggled to free himself. It was no use. The steel shackles held him inside the doomed cart.

The ride neared the mouth. Batman braced himself for the blow.

The machine's giant teeth clamped down onto the back of the cart. They crunched through the metal like a pretzel. Just as quickly, the clown's mouth opened up again.

The teeth had barely missed Batman's hands. The bolts of one of his shackles had come loose. Batman freed his right hand. He grabbed three mini Bat-grenades from his Utility Belt.

Batman looked up. The clown's teeth were closing again. Quickly, Batman placed the small explosives on the rest of the shackles. Then he pressed *Fire*.

POP! POP! POP! The mini grenades blasted through the locks.

Batman was free. But it was too late. The angry teeth of the clown machine were closing down again. Batman had to act quickly.

"I hope you're hungry!" he yelled at the giant machine. Then he jumped into the throat of the deadly clown.

Batman tumbled down the dark tunnel that led from the clown mouth. He tried to stop himself by digging his gloves into the walls. Sparks flew from his fingertips. He fell deeper and deeper.

A light at the end of the tunnel got closer. An instant later, Batman shot out of the tube like a bullet.

He slammed onto the floor of a large, empty room.

"Did you enjoy the ride?! HAHAHAHA!" said a loud voice from above.

Batman looked up toward the ceiling. He spotted the Joker. The Joker was standing in a spotlight on a balcony above him.

"Not as much as I'll enjoy seeing you behind bars," replied Batman. He struggled to his feet.

"That's very funny. But I'm the one who makes the jokes around here," yelled the Joker. "Now perhaps you'd like to play a little game!"

"What do I win?" asked Batman.

The Joker laughed. "You should be more worried about what you're going to lose," he said. The Joker pulled on a long rope that dangled beside him.

Suddenly, two doors on the ceiling swung open. Batman watched a hundred red and green balloons spill out of the opening. Slowly, they floated down toward him.

"Balloons?" said Batman, puzzled.

"Not just any balloons," said the Joker. "The green ones are full of the most poisonous gas on earth. If one of them pops, **POOF!** It's bye, bye, Bat!"

The Joker pulled three large darts out of his pocket. The pointy tips shined in the spotlight.

"If you're lucky, this game will be over soon," said the Joker.

He threw a dart toward the balloons. **POP!** The first dart popped a single red balloon. Then it landed on the floor.

"Drat!" yelled the Joker. "Time for round two!"

The Joker wound up like a major league pitcher. He tossed the second dart. This time, the dart headed right for a group of green balloons.

Batman grabbed a Batarang from his Utility Belt. He threw it into the air. **CHING!** The Batarang hit the dart. It knocked the dart off course, sending it into the wall.

"No fair! No fair! No fair!" the Joker screamed from the balcony.

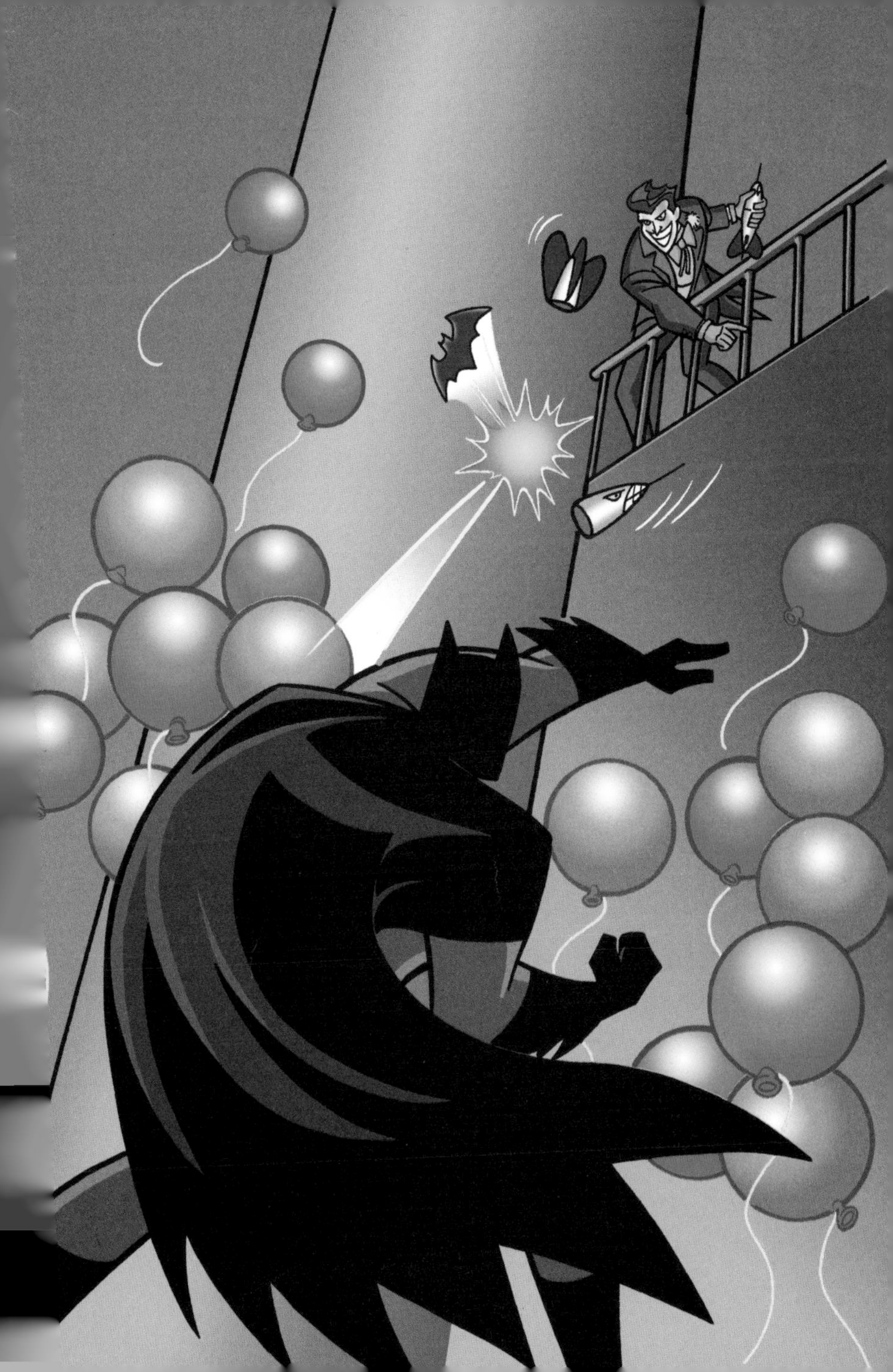

The Joker jumped up and down. He stomped his feet in anger.

"You never told me the rules," replied Batman.

"No matter," said the Joker, winding up again. "I have one dart left. It's all I need to get rid of you."

The Joker threw the final dart. Just as quickly, Batman leaped into the air. He twirled around in circles like a giant fan. The burst of wind scattered the balloons in every direction. Batman landed. He watched the final dart stick into the floor.

"Looks like the game's over, Clown," said Batman.

"That's where you're wrong, Batman!" screamed the Joker. "This game is just beginning."

The Joker reached behind him. He picked up a large bucket. Batman could see that the bucket was filled with darts. With a terrible laugh, the Joker dumped the bucket over the balcony. Then he ran out of the room. Hundreds of darts rained down toward the balloons below.

Batman knew he couldn't stop them all. He reached for his gun that shot grappling hooks. He aimed and fired it toward the balcony. The hook swirled around the balcony railing and clamped tight.

Batman held onto the gun. As the grappling hook's cord wound back into the gun, Batman soared into the air. He shielded himself against the falling darts with his cape.

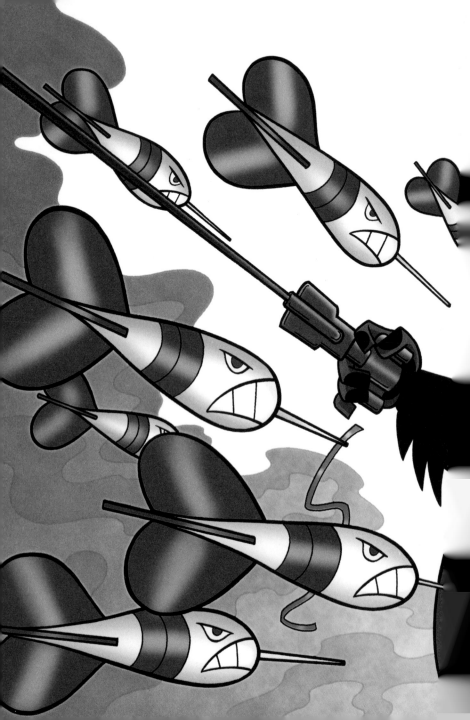

Below him, a hundred red and green balloons exploded. **POP! POP! POP!** Batman watched as a cloud of deadly gas filled the room.

Without a moment to lose, Batman flipped onto the balcony. Then he rushed through the open doorway.

Batman was safe . . . for now.

CHAPTER 4

ROBOT CLOWNS

Batman ran down a dark tunnel. He hoped the Joker hadn't gotten away. Soon, Batman reached a long wooden bridge. It shook from side to side with every step. At the end of the bridge, a dizzying black and white disc spun around and around like a pinwheel.

Batman lost his footing. His boot slipped between the bridge's wooden boards. He caught himself and looked down. Far below, he saw an inky black moat. It was filled with a thousand angry piranhas.

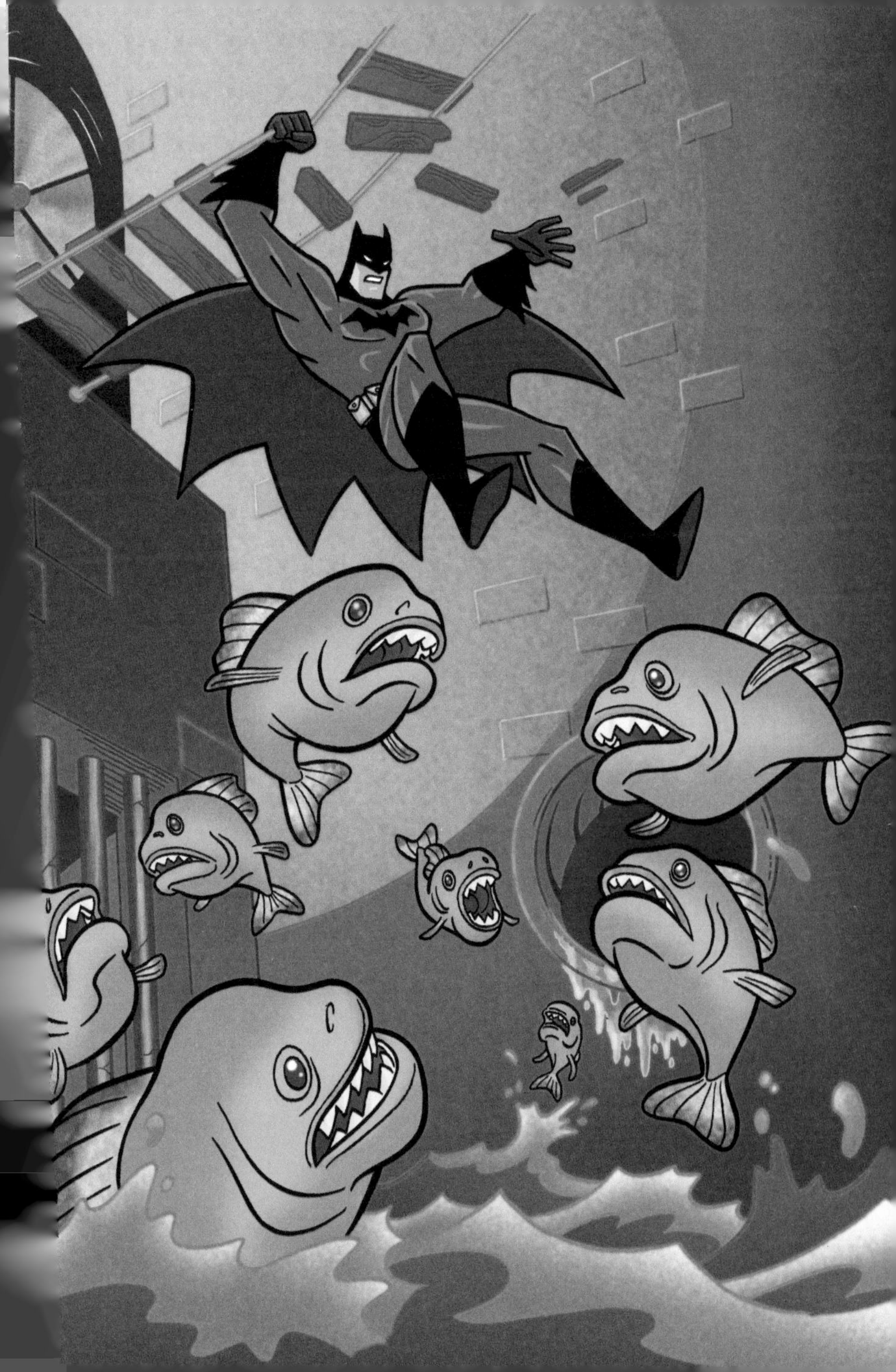

The tiny fish held their mouths in the air. They chomped with hunger and waited for their next juicy meal.

MUNCH! MUNCH! MUNCH!

Whew! The Joker nearly turned me into fish food, Batman thought. He picked himself up. He sprinted across the rest of the bridge. Passing through the swirling tunnel, Batman entered another dark room.

"Nice work, Batman!" The Joker's voice echoed through the darkness. "But the fun ends here!"

Suddenly, the lights flipped on. Batman swirled around. He looked in every direction. A hundred Jokers surrounded him. Their evil, white faces laughed wildly.

"Give up, Batman! You can't defeat us all!" screamed the group of a hundred Jokers.

With a grim smile, Batman recalled the carnival his parents took him to on his birthday. They had walked through a fun house. He remembered holding his father's hand when they entered the area called the House of Mirrors. Inside, dozens of mirrors repeated his reflection around the room.

"A simple trick!" Batman yelled. "Only one of these images is real! I won't stop until I find you, Joker!"

Batman jumped toward one of the laughing Jokers. With a swift kick, the glass shattered into a thousand pieces. But it wasn't a mirror after all. It was a glass case.

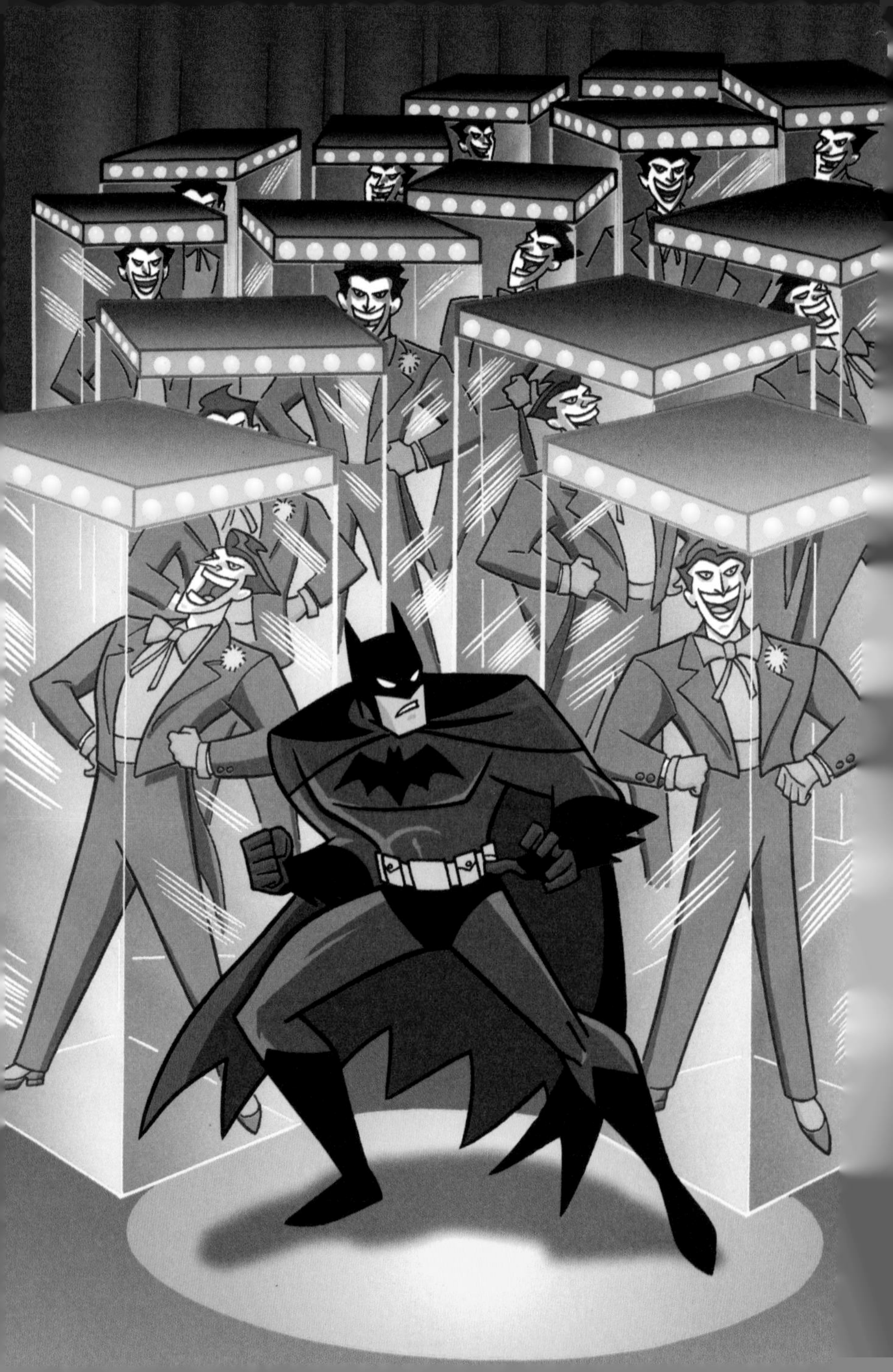

Inside the case stood a clone of the
Joker. Batman walked toward the clone.
He grabbed its green hair and pulled. A
white rubber mask came off in his hand.

"Robots!" Batman yelled. He stared
into the clone's metal face.

"That's right!" the hundred angry
Jokers replied. "An army of them!"

Suddenly, the rest of the Joker robots
crashed through their glass cases. They
held their arms out like zombies and
marched into a line.

Then the real Joker stepped out from
the shadows. He stood in front of his robot
troops and laughed.

"I knew the mask at the asylum would lead you here, Batman!" yelled the Joker. "Now my army of robots will destroy you once and for all!"

"The joke's on you, Joker," replied Batman.

"What do you mean?" the Joker sneered.

"You knew the chemicals in the mask would lead me here? Then you should have known that they're also very flammable!" Batman continued.

"Huh?" Joker said, frowning.

Batman grabbed his last mini Bat-grenade from the side of his Utility Belt. He tossed it into the crowd of robots. The countdown timer began to beep.

BEEP! BEEP! BEEP!

Then Batman fired one of his grappling guns into the air. The hook stuck into the ceiling. The cable tightened. As it wound back into the gun, Batman was pulled into the air.

"No! Noooooooooo!" the Joker yelled.

Hanging from the ceiling, Batman looked down at his evil enemy. His Bat-grenade beeped louder and faster. It was about to explode.

"You didn't think I'd forget you, did you Joker?" said Batman. He pulled out another grappling gun with his other hand. He fired it toward the Joker. The cord swirled around him and tied itself in a knot. Batman pushed the *Recoil* button on the gun. The Joker soared up toward Batman, kicking and screaming.

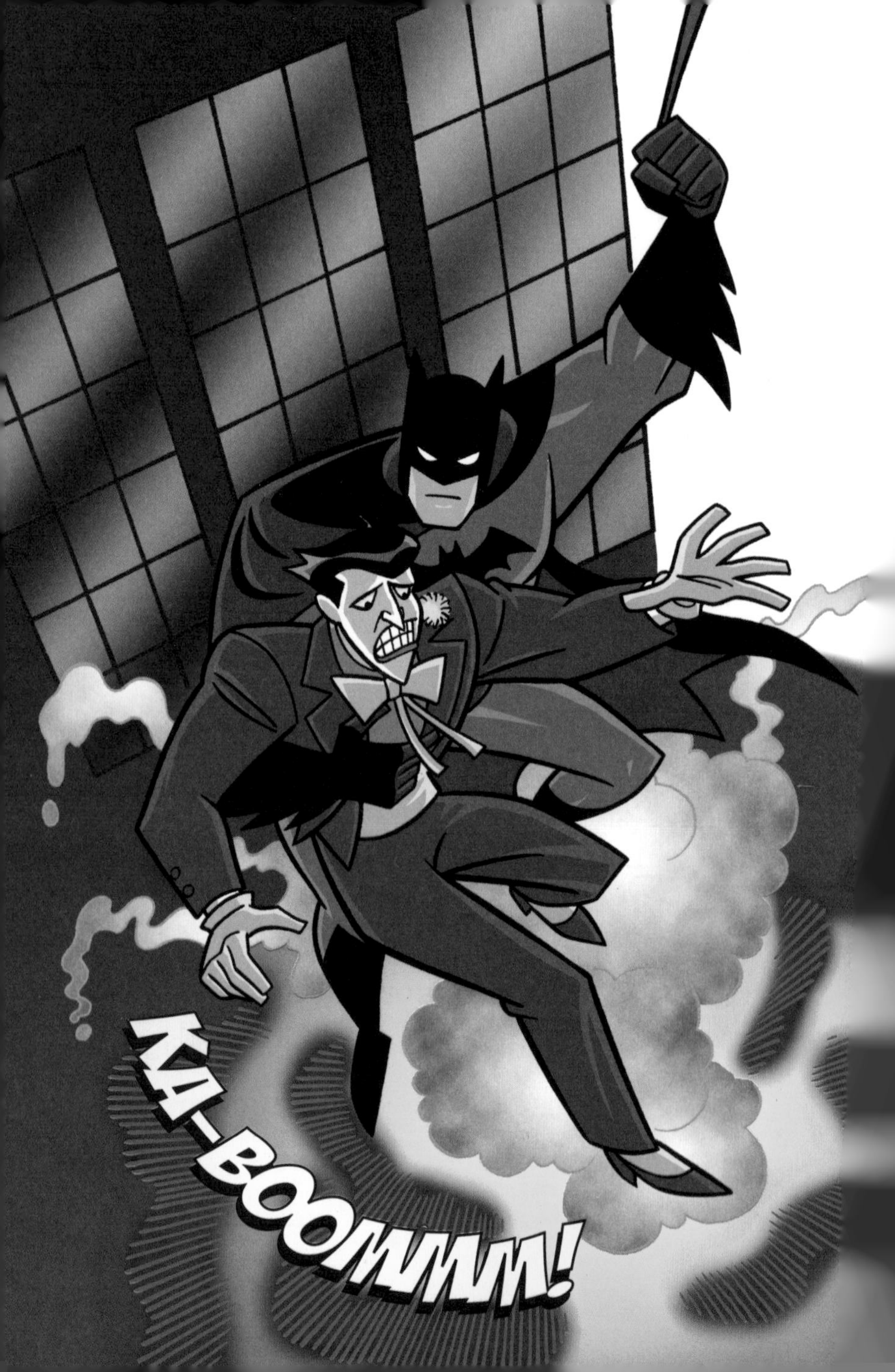
KA-BOOMMM!

The mini Bat-grenade exploded. The hundred Joker robots burst into flames. A giant fireball rose toward the ceiling. Batman wrapped his cape around himself and the Joker. He shielded them both from the heat.

"You can thank me later," said Batman. The Joker continued to kick and scream.

CHAPTER 5

THE GIFT OF JUSTICE

Later that evening at Wayne Manor, Alfred, the butler, sat in the den. He was enjoying a cup of tea. Suddenly, Alfred heard noises coming from Bruce Wayne's bedroom. Fearing the worst, he grabbed the poker from the fireplace. He crept slowly down the hallway.

Alfred peeked inside the bedroom doorway. He saw Bruce sitting quietly in his evening chair. He was looking at the picture of his parents again.

"Master Bruce! I didn't hear you come in," exclaimed Alfred.

Bruce turned and looked over his shoulder. He saw Alfred standing in the doorway.

"Hello, Alfred," Bruce replied. "I just returned moments ago."

"Can I get you anything, sir?" asked Alfred.

"No thank you," said Bruce.

"Very well," Alfred said. He turned to leave, but stopped. "And how was your birthday, sir, if you don't mind me asking?"

"One of the best," said Bruce. He glanced back at the picture. "I got just what I wanted."

Back across town at Arkham Asylum, Commissioner Gordon and the Gotham City Police continued their investigation. Suddenly, two of the asylum's guards rushed out of the building.

"Commissioner! Commissioner!" the startled guards yelled, pointing toward the asylum's front doors. "There's something inside that you have to see!"

The Commissioner followed the guards inside the asylum. They walked quickly down the long corridor of cells. Angry prisoners hooted and howled as they passed by.

At the end of the hallway, the guards unlocked a series of large, steel doors. The doors led into the maximum-security wing of the prison.

When they unlocked the final door, Commissioner Gordon stood frozen in shock.

On the floor of a locked prison cell lay the Joker. His hands and feet were tied together with thick, red ribbon. A giant red bow was stuck neatly on top of his head.

The Joker twisted, turned, and struggled to get loose. He moaned through a piece of tape that covered his mouth.

"Remove the tape," ordered Commissioner Gordon.

The guard slowly approached the Joker. He grabbed the piece of tape and yanked it off with one swift pull. This time, the evil, white face beneath the tape wasn't a mask.

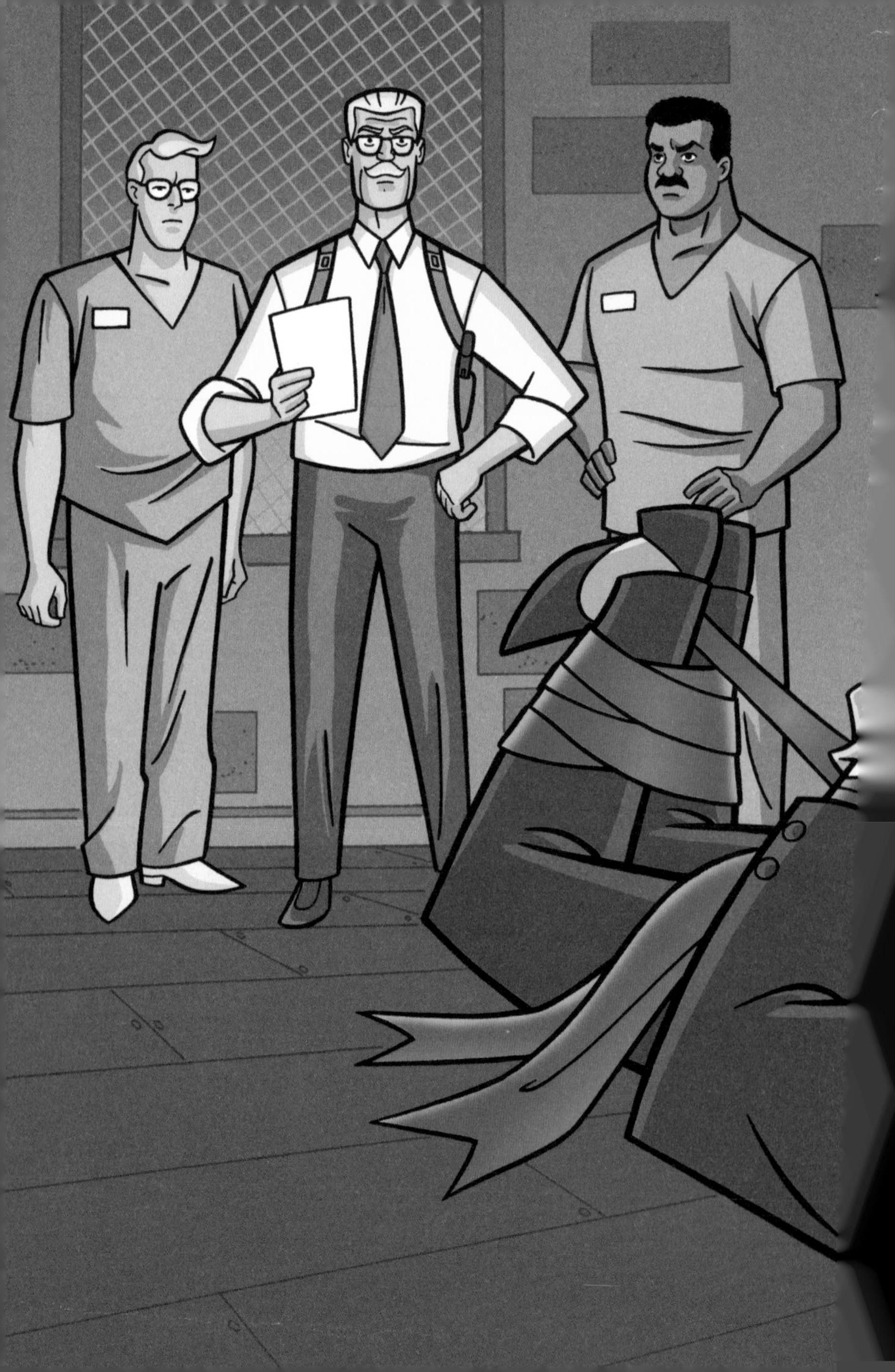

"I'll get you for this, Batman!" yelled the Joker. "I'll get you!!"

The Clown Prince of Crime was back behind bars. It was the perfect birthday gift for Batman, the world's greatest crime fighter. Justice.

Joker, The

REAL NAME: Jack Napier

OCCUPATION: Professional Criminal

BASE: Gotham City

HEIGHT:
6 feet 5 inches

WEIGHT:
192 pounds

EYES:
Green

HAIR:
Green

The Clown Prince of Crime. The Harlequin of Hate. The Ace of Knaves. Batman's most dangerous enemy is known by many names, but he answers to no one. After falling into a vat of toxic waste, this once lowly criminal was transformed into an evil madman. The chemical bath bleached his skin, dyed his hair green, and peeled back his lips into a permanent grin. Since then, the Joker has only one purpose in life . . . to destroy Batman. In the meantime, however, he's happy tormenting the good people of Gotham.

G.C.P.D. GOTHAM CITY POLICE DEPARTMENT

- The Joker always wants the last laugh. To get it, he's devised dozens of deadly clown tricks. He has even gone as far as faking his own death!

- Always the trickster, the Joker designs all of his weapons to look comical in order to conceal their true danger. This trickery usually gets a chuckle or two from his foes, giving the Joker an opportunity to strike first.

- The Clown Prince of Crime has spent more time in Arkham Asylum than any Gotham criminal. But that doesn't mean he's comfortable behind bars. He has also escaped more times than anyone.

- While at Arkham, the Joker met Dr. Harleen Quinzel. She fell madly in love and aided the crazy clown in his many escapes. Soon, she turned to a life of crime herself, as the evil jester Harley Quinn.

CONFIDENTIAL

BIOGRAPHIES

Donald Lemke works as a children's book editor. He is the author of the Zinc Alloy graphic novel adventure series. He also wrote *Captured Off Guard*, a World War II story, and a graphic novelization of *Gulliver's Travels*, both of which were selected by the Junior Library Guild.

Erik Doescher is a freelance illustrator and video game designer based in Dallas, Texas. He attended the School of Visual Arts in New York City. Erik illustrated for a number of comic studios throughout the 1990s, and then moved to Texas to pursue videogame development and design. However, he has not completely given up on illustrating his favorite comic book characters.

Mike DeCarlo is a longtime contributor of comic art whose range extends from Batman and Iron Man to Bugs Bunny and Scooby-Doo. He resides in Connecticut with his wife and four children.

David Tanguay has over 20 years of experience in the comic book industry, including work as an editor, layout artist, colorist, and letterer. He also has worked in web design and taught computer graphics at the State University of New York.

 GLOSSARY

afterburner (AF-tur-bur-ner)—a device used to increase the speed of something

asylum (uh-SYE-luhm)—a hospital for the mentally ill

ballroom (BAWL-room)—a very large room where parties and dances are held

clone (KLOHN)—a copy of something

flammable (FLAM-uh-buhl)—if something is flammable, it can easily catch fire

moat (MOHT)—a deep, wide ditch filled with water that is used to defend against intruders

piranhas (pir-RAH-nuhz)—small, vicious, meat-eating fish

recoil (ree-KOIL)—if you recoil something, you wind something up to bring it back toward you

transformation (trans-for-MAY-shuhn)—a change into something else

Utility Belt (yoo-TIL-uh-tee BELT)—Batman's belt, which holds all of his weaponry and gadgets

DISCUSSION QUESTIONS

1. In this book, the Joker tries to destroy Batman with angry piranhas, poisonous balloons, and robot clones. Why do you think Batman still saves the Joker from the explosion? Would you have done the same?

2. Billionaire Bruce Wayne is secretly Batman. Why do you think he keeps his identity a secret? If you were a super hero, would you tell anyone?

3. At the end of the story, the Joker is back behind bars at Arkham Asylum. Do you think he'll escape again? Why or why not?

WRITING PROMPTS

1. The Joker's Fun House of Evil is filled with dozens of terrifying rides and games. Write about some of the scariest or most exciting rides you've ever been on.

2. Write your own story about Batman and the Joker. How will the Joker escape from Arkham Asylum? Will Batman capture him again, or will the Joker get away? You decide.

3. In this book, Bruce Wayne had a pretty crazy birthday. Write a story about your craziest birthday ever. Where did you go? What gifts did you receive?

MORE NEW BATMAN ADVENTURES!

EMPEROR OF THE AIRWAVES

THE FOG OF FEAR

THE REVENGE OF CLAYFACE

POISON IVY'S DEADLY GARDEN

FIVE RIDDLES FOR ROBIN

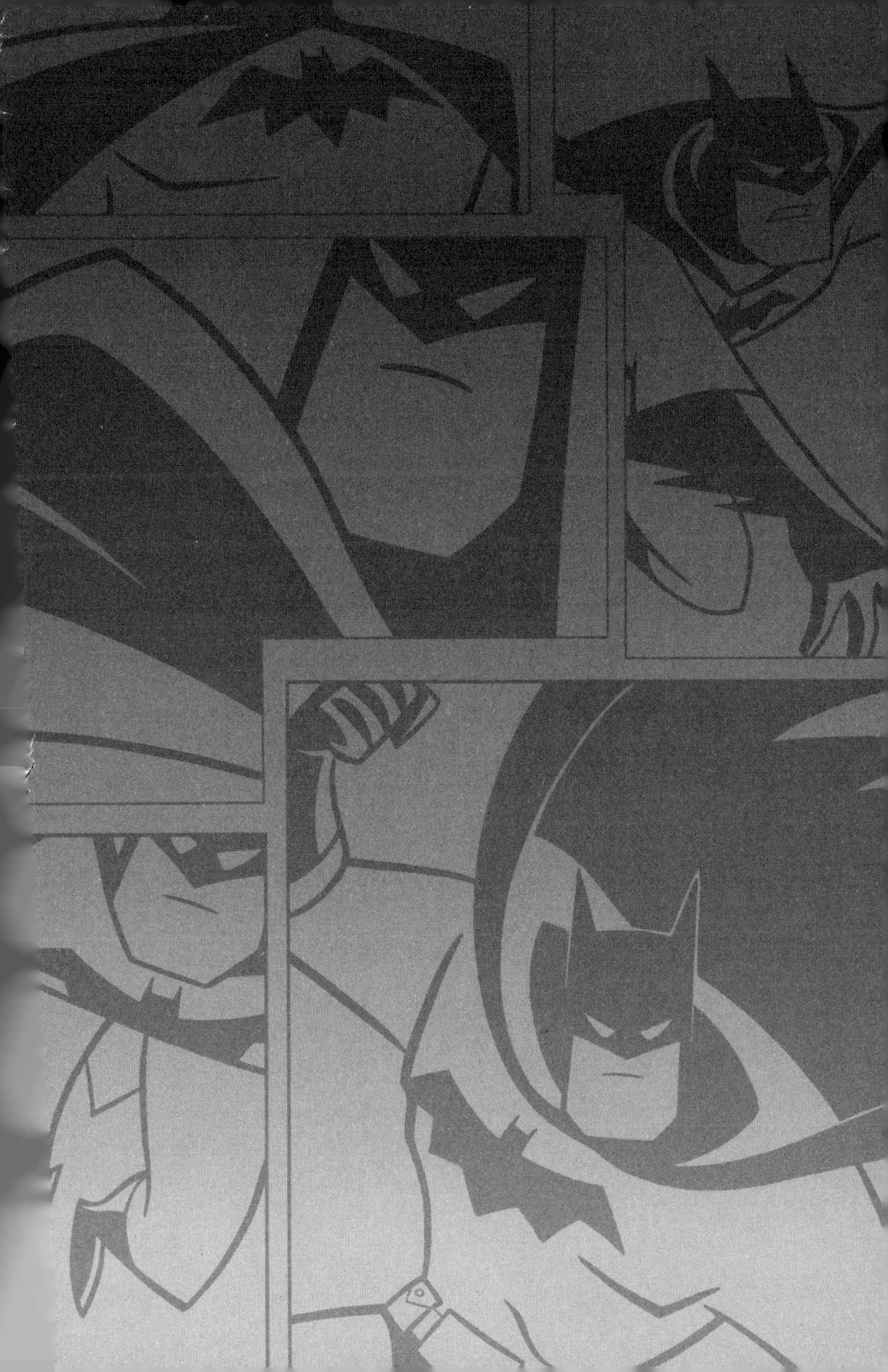

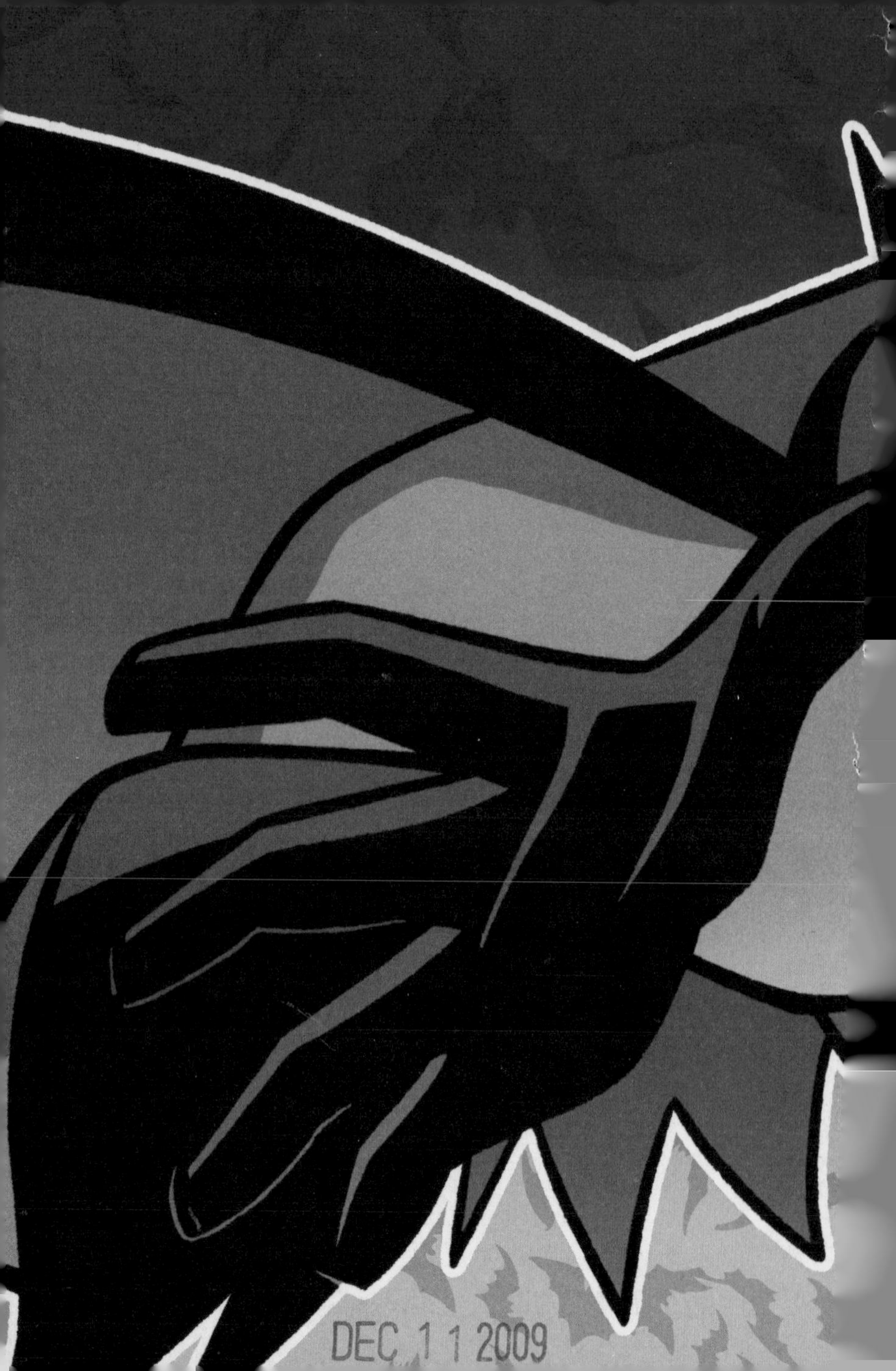